Remembering Yesterdays Imagining Tomorrows

POETRY COLLECTION

BURT E. PRINGLE

Printed in the United States of America 2012.

A cataloguing record for this book that includes the U.S. Library of Congress Classification number, the Library of Congress Call number and the Dewey Decimal cataloguing code.

ISBN: 978-1-4269-3047-8 (sc)

Library of Congress Control Number: 2010905812

Order this book online at www.trafford.com
or email orders@trafford.com

Most Trafford titles are also available at major online book retailers.

 www.trafford.com

North America & international
toll-free: 1 888 232 4444 (USA & Canada)
phone: 250 383 6864 ♦ fax: 812 355 4082

TO MY MOTHER
1909–1929

My mother my creator.
She held the seed that bore me.
As I grew inside her womb,
she nourished me
and gave me strength.
Through her, I inherited the past.
From her, I became the future.
My prayer. That I have proven
worthy of her pain and love.

From my second book
"Love and Summer Days Fade Away"

"Always write first things
utmost in the heart."
Edgar Allen Poe
1809–1849

A NOTE FROM THE AUTHOR

You may find that my poetry reflects my
real and imaginary past, present, and future.
Some poems are more direct, personal or
reflective of the times, therefore I write about
the human condition in several voices --- as an
observer, as a lover, the forlorn: exploring
fantasies and making social comments.
Poetry expresses my thoughts on love, desires
and anticipation, loss and departing, with hope
for the unseen tomorrow.
So I shall write and sincerely hope in some way
my efforts will entertain, enlighten or inform
--- maybe heal.

What a luxury late in life to be in love, and
assured that your peace of mind prevails.

All of us have questions, ever those that are
unanswerable.
God has the answers.

Sincerely
Burt

TITLE OF THIS COLLECTION is a line from my poem
I ONCE WAS THERE in Book 2 LOVE and SUMMER DAYS
FADE AWAY page 65.

COVER PHOTOGRAPH. My mother at a young age
with a friend named Gerg.

I extend my heart–felt thanks to
Ms. Bronwen Chandler
for her expertise and assistance in the editing
of this collection of my poetry.

I would also like to thank
all the people
who have come into my life
and have joined hands
to encircle me.

CONTENT..

"Let us read and let us dance
--- two amusements that will never
do any harm to the world."
Voltaire
1694–1778

WANING

Wandering like the moon.
I follow in its path
only to return
to the same place again
the next night
a little less visible.

MOMENTS AND MEMORIES

Time takes away
*   our moments*
*   and leaves us*
*   with their memories.*
Hold dear, and cherish
*   the bliss that your love*
*   has known.*

*

MEMORIES RETURN

He came home
but could not stay:
too many memories
of yesterday.

I ONCE WAS THERE *

I love you now my morning star.
I love you when night shades fall.
It is when you are in my arms,
I love you most of all.

I see you again, then you leave
and once more I bid you
a fond adieu.
Remembering yesterdays
--- imagining tomorrows.

Come hold me close my darling
and tell me that you care.
I may not get to Heaven when I die.
I'm happy knowing, with you
--- I once was there.

*From my second book "LOVE and SUMMER DAYS
FADE AWAY" page 65

MUSIC OF THE WORLD

The world is made of music
if you can only stop to hear:
the song of the wind
moving through the trees
and across the rustling grasses:
the rhythm of the ocean and its waves
as they play their tune brushing the shore:
the cosmic melodies that spur
the stars to dance.

Hear that lyrical breath of air floating across
a rippling brook or the waters of a spring
bubbling into existence.
Hear the bird's song, the frog's croak,
the bee's hum and the roosters crow.

Celebrate the earth in concert
as celestial music passes through the night
and the days play out their symphony:
even stillness has its own special
melodic awareness.

I hope I never grow too old to enjoy
the music of the world.

NOW IT'S OUR TURN

We deserve to be young again
in our golden years.
It has been a joyful experience
--- the journey to this age.

The wheat is in harvest.
We've been through the mill,
the flour made and the bread baked.

Now it's our turn.

To love and touch love once more
--- to ride the winds and carousels.
Gather friends and flowers
and kick up our heels.
Instead, they want us to "act our age,"
put us in a rocker somewhere
away from the light.
But, this is not going to happen.
We're going to rock all right
--- with a little roll,
and we're not afraid of the light
--- we're not fading.

We're going to dance and sing,
run hand–in–hand in the rain,
chase rainbows and challenge this life
until the sun sets --- then watch–out
as we rip through the night
in celebration.

Now it's our turn.

MIDNIGHT WALTZ

The magic of the midnight hour
makes their senses soar
as they dance to the wind and its song
rustling through the trees
of a leaf–laden forest floor.

The moon, full and mellow,
looks down to see
their reflections silhouetted
in the lake below.
Two hearts embrace in love,
to be free in heart and spirit
 --- free as the air to twirl,
while waltzing at midnight
 --- a dance they both adore.

The magic of the midnight hour
makes their senses soar
as they dance to the wind and its song
rustling through the trees
of a leaf–laden forest floor.

CONFETTI DANCING

The sullen sky speaks
of things to come.
Autumn leaves trickle down
like confetti, blanketing the ground.
Variegated hues of colour
--- browns, yellows, oranges,
splashed with grays, black and red.
Summer fading,
waltzing to the song of autumn.

A season of happiness was his to hold.
Love and joy once sang from his heart
--- now his life wrapped in loneliness,
cloaked in sorrow with a broken heart
and broken promises at the end of the ride.
She will never know the richness
this love would have brought forth.

As shadows fell across the night,
the last leaf pirouettes
leaving un–canopied trees
--- and a heart buried
in love's lonely grave.

AUTUMN CORNFIELD

The billowing clouds
ride on a new day sky.
The harvest over, the corn,
hung in the storehouse to dry,
while tiny field mice scamper
to hide from a sky hawk's
roving eye.

The winds of change
cause the barren stalks
to dance --- as autumn comes
to make its annual call.

Now the field will be cut
in many complicated ways,
and a tired 'ole scarecrow
will invite you in to play
in the newly formed
cornfield maze.

DWELLING THOUGHTS

As life's flame dims
--- its ashes fill our hearth,
and the cold of night draws nearer,
we'll sit in age with quickened hearts
watching long shadows
dance across the room
and sequesterly remember
the radiant days of our summers:
when the bloom was on the rose
and the jessamine's scent filled the air
and we delighted in the daffodil's
yellow glow as we walked the promenade
under a southern sky.

We will remember when
the blaze of our love bloomed
like the flowers in the field,
and all the vows we made
and cherish still.

My thoughts still dwell on you my love,
--- my thoughts still dwell on you.
And when I close my eyes in final night
my thoughts will be of you.

YESTERDAYS

Let me fill my days
with yesterdays
for they hold all
the memories of you.

Ever since I lost you
--- I have lost my way.
Even the night—clouds
hang about me
all through the day.

There were dreams
lost over time,
for life was cruel
and crushed
our love divine.

So let me fill my days
with yesterdays
for they echo
the music of you.

SIREN SONG

I long to hear once more
my mermaid's song
as she sat on a sea—swept rock
to serenade me.

A bewitching beauty
with necklace of black pearls,
her golden tresses
cascading over her shoulders
adorned with shells and starfish
to cover her voluptuous breast.
The iridescent blue—green scales
of her flip—flopping tail
--- fascinating me.
Her feminine wiles,
her innate beauty,
her soft, smooth flesh
--- entrancing me.

Sunken treasures could not
--- would not intrigue me.
But her sweet song
could lure me far below
the salt air, the waves, the sea,
where I would grow gills
to join my sea nymph in the depth
of her undersea realm
among the bright pink coral
and seaweed.

SILENT PICTURES, SILENT MEMORIES

When I was a little tot, my Grandmother
would place me on her lap
at the kitchen table and open a big book
full of images held in place by tiny tabs
from the "Five and Dime" so they won't
escape their big black prison.
A book full of silent pictures
* --- silent memories.*
Yesterday's memories caught,
collected and saved to ponder in age
* --- memories forgotten*
if not for the thoughtful camera.
Life brought to stillness
in black and white, some in colour,
even a few "tin types" from long ago,
and those the instant camera recorded.
All placed in iconographical order
to tell a story of people, places,
and growing up.
Views of vacations long forgot, and,
who's that standing next to Aunt Frances ?
Relatives gone and those who survived.

A little white flower pressed between
the pages, she said, "that is Edel Weiss"
as if I knew Edel Weiss from Unkle Fred.

>>

Odd that Dad and Grandpa
seems to have always stepped out
of the picture frame --- except
for a few snap shots.

Now we flash projected images
on a wall (big as life), and then
tuck them away in a little yellow box
for safe keeping
 --- the whole family tucked away
in a single grave.

Then we leave to our own grave
with the children and grand children
scavenging through our belongings
for a favorite memento, a photograph
to keep, cherish and remind them
that we were here
 --- just before the estate sale.

NO TIME FOR BLUES

In the dark of night,
through street–light shadows
they followed the sounds of the city
down into the "Quarter."

It was summer and hot
at the "Jack of Clubs"
where he raised his horn
to play the blues,
but jazz came rushing forth
 --- no time for blues.
The drummer, dismayed,
his steel brushes he laid,
and with his "pounding the skins"
brought the beat into play.
The piano–man's fingers
now flying across the keys.
The sax–man hurled
his mournful tones
into shrieks, squeaks and trills.
The deep riffs of a trombone
with its slide moving in and out,
penetrating the thick air
 --- and big base slappin'
like you've never heard before
 --- no time for blues.

>>

The club now dim,
some patrons hang around
as the musicians gather
for the "after–set" at 2am
 --- a gig only jazz lovers
could understand.

Spent cigarette smoke, overflowing
ash trays and slightly filled
booze glasses everywhere
 --- the vibes still fill the room.
Sweat–filled brows, parched lips
and sore fingers, yet all is silent
except the surge of music.
Then a "bird" stepped into the light
separating sound from smoke
with her deep, scratched throat,
and 'scat' sang in a verbiage all her own.
Sitting there the sounds melt
into your soul.
They closed the night at 5am,
then rushed away for another
cigarette, morning drink,
and to bed.

Bourbon Street has never
been the same since the night
it too absorbed that sound.
No more time for blues --- because
the jazz starts again at 6pm
for the tourist trade.

CITY SHADOWS, CITY LIGHTS

Long shadows creep across the city,
across the New York skyline,
and down the hustling and bustling
canyons at eventide.
Then they slip away into oblivion
as the towering lights begin to shine
and dazzle in the night.
Night life in the city affords a chance
to unleash the stresses and traumas
of the day; to go and find the luxuries
that prevail.
Manhattan, with the UN peacefully
resting on its eastern shore.
Grand Central with a myriad
of strangers, mingling and passing
in the night.
Madison with the after—business bars
and galleries.
Streams of yellow taxis
streaking the streets, up 5ᵗʰ, down 7ᵗʰ
--- but try to catch one in the rain.
Strolling down Broadway
with all the glitter and glare
--- no chance for shadows here.
Taking in all the wonders, sights
and sounds of that neon cave.

>>

You can taste the air filled with haze
--- the steaming grates,
in the now rain–swept streets.
The delightful smells from street vendors
--- the open fast food stands
and see the "night girls"
                    flaunting their wares.
Hitting the high spots --- the arcades,
the taverns, the clubs.
Taking in theater
--- it sends you into a trance with all its
drama, music and dance.

So, what will the next sunrise bring ?

Come morning,
as the night lights dim,
and the skyline's long shadows
stretch across the Hudson,
you can still see "her eternal light"
shining across the bay.

THE MARK OF TIME

Time leaves its mark
on all of us.
With faded memories
and broken dreams,
furrowed faces,
withered hands
and silvered hair.
We remove life's mask
in waning years
for all to witness
our true selves
--- longing for serenity
in our lives
--- peace for our souls.

We open our hearts to receive
tenderness and care
as we walk those
last lingering miles.

We grasp at the sunset
that will take us
into final darkness
--- only to wake once more
in God's new morning light.

DEAF–DEFYING
To Nancy

On the eve of her 60th birthday
she had not lost any of her beauty,
but the sounds around her
were growing dim.

Ears perked to receive
every word that was aired.
Her love of music
 --- becoming impaired.

Not to be defeated
 --- not wanting everything repeated,
she took measures to rectify
Nature's little glitch.
Everything now more intense,
her voice fuller
 --- has a richer pitch.

The sounds of life
still stir her passion (to hear).

"Isn't it strange that
 --- until it's too late,
we hear without listening
and listen without hearing."
Pringle

THAT INNER ATTIC

Secrets held back
in a drafty and darkened attic
  --- looming somewhere in your mind.
Walls cracked from pain
  --- drenched with tears
of sorrow and regret.
Musty smells of the past
are everywhere.
Lost loves and heartaches
collected and stored
in memory boxes on the floor
  --- now overgrown with life's
cobwebs and lies
as molecules of dust dance
in the dim light from a window
that views only despair.

Only you can find the key
to unlock the door
  --- escape depression
and your inner attic.

NOWHERE TRAIN

The faces in the station, familiar,
yet you have never met.
All strangers passing in the night
taking the midnight train
to nowhere, a place no one can explain
                    --- ALL ABOARD !

The cadence of the wheels
with their clickity, clack
is the heartbeat of the night.
Emptiness rides the rails
through eerie tunnels
and strange passages
and the lights are dim at every crossing.
The tracks narrow, reaching into infinity
 --- yet infinity never arrives.

Life captured in darkness,
in a place where disconnected thoughts,
forgotten memories
and lost dreams dwell.
Where loneliness and despair
are the unseen ghosts that prowl the night,
and are the nightmares
your life has to endure.

Midnight train, destination unknown
                    --- ALL ABOARD !

AMARANTHINE

On fruitful days
in all swiftness
did I pursue her,
for we know not
what each day will bring
at the wakening
of a new dawn.

I long for the promises
gleaming on her lips,
the pools of passion
deep in her eyes,
 --- to embrace the intoxication
and the ecstasy.

Naked I wait, defenseless,
with tormented soul
and smitten heart
 --- I find no sleep
for in my life
she is my amaranthine.

"Life is weary and tiresome"[1]
at love's broken fountain
where sweet tears freely flow
in the dank of night
from a heart bereaven.

>>

Yet my unfailing love for her
"I cherish more than life itself" [2]
--- nothing will set this love apart
for she is my heart's flower
that will never fade.

[1] Ecclesiastes 1:8–9
"Life is weary and tiresome
no matter how much I pursue."

[2] Psalms 63

Burt Quote:
"Find the flower of your dreams
and cultivate it's beauty. "

ADAM

I woke one morning in the dust.
The mist was heavy and I could not see
the sunrise through my dreamy eyes.
I woke to find an aching side
and a creature like me, but different,
lying beside me, soft and warm.
Then a voice spoke through the clouds
telling me this is my companion,
my mate to enjoy the fruits
of the garden and the union,
warning us not to partake
of a certain tree.
All was fine. Then one day
a deceptive voice from a slitherer
convinced us there was no fear
if we wanted to take from that tree
and we plucked its fruit.
It was tasty and refreshing
but filled us with pain.

Then thunder began to roar,
clouds turned black, the wind came up
and drove us out of the garden.
We shivered from the cold and found
how different we were; and ran
from each other, making garments
to cover our nakedness.
God told us we didn't keep the faith.
The serpent and temptation
led us astray; now we must live forever
outside the garden.

GARDEN OF LOST DREAMS

The garden left unattended
--- the sun has had its way.
His rose has withered
--- turned cold and gray,
for time has taken
the bloom away.

It was a love built on trust,
now everything beautiful
has turned to dust.
No more pain
--- no more tears.
All hope abandoned
through the years.

The garden still washed
by moonlight
--- the same stars
stretch across the sky.
So what has brought him here
after all this time ?
Sitting there reminiscing
--- sipping wine,
like nothing else has changed.

Now the "un–dreaming" must begin
--- for only mushrooms grow
in darkness.

ULTIMATE JOY / CONSTANT PAIN

She charmed his heart --- cast a spell
that can not be broken.
Yet there are unspoken words
locked in her heart.

If he could only change the time,
close the distance --- a beginning
without end between two hearts,
letting passion be their guide, rule their days,
transcending all thoughts of logic.

All adversities could have been
their stepping stones --- a path
they could have shared.
A chance to feed their hopes and dreams
--- time would have allowed to endure.

She was never more cherished.
She was never more loved.

She was his state–of–mind,
his life, his joy, his love
during his insanity.

It is going to be hard for him
to open his heart again --- very hard,
for love can be the ultimate joy
or a continual source of pain !

NOT CLOSE ENOUGH TO TOUCH

Sometimes at morning—rise
you can see the moon's
full white sphere
trying to reach its beloved sun
--- for it revels in its warmth
and loving glow.
Traveling in a cloud of remorse
--- always coming close
but not connecting.

This longing heart of mine
knows the moon's dilemma:
trying to reach a heart
that is always near,
but not close enough
to touch.

JACKSONVILLE SUNRISE

Driving to work
  during the early morning
    rush hour,
    the sun's coming up
  behind me.
Its golden glow
  illumes the
  towering structures
    of the city
  that pierce the low–lying fog
  while the darkness
  and stillness below
  are broken
    by the glaring headlights
    and pulsating sounds
    of traffic.

WAITING FOR THE SUNRISE

It's early morning
in the city,
but my mind is transported
to the country
when a neighbor's
pet rooster
breaks the silence
and starts to crow.

It fills the air
with a peacefulness
as if I were really there,
waiting for the sunrise,
to go and gather eggs.

VESSEL OF CLAY

She came and filled my life
with joy.
She broke my solitude
--- took away my sleep.
Yet, I still dream.

I unwrapped the bonds
that bound me
--- removed the chains
that restrained me
and opened my vulnerable heart.

She is one of God's vessels,
made by His own hands
--- from clay.

Let me fill her with love.

ALONE
To my mother,

The night she gave
*   birth to me*
*   her heart was filled*
*   with love.*

Suddenly,
*   the light was gone*
*   as deaths shadow*
*   passed her eyes*
*   and I was left alone.*

Every night in prayer
*   I thank her for this life*
*   and her sacrifice.*
For now, I am alone.

I hear her whispers
*   in my night–dreams*
*   --- they dry my eyes,*
*   and calm my fears.*
For now, I live alone.

And when I am
*   once again*
*   in her loving arms*
*   no more will I be alone.*

INVITATION

Stroll with me
these next few years
and we will find
happiness together.

Stroll with me
along a strand
of sparkling sand
to wade at water's edge
as we take in another
golden sunset
that will precede
all our enchanted nights.

Come stroll with me
my darling
 --- stroll with me.

HEART TEARS

Unable to touch his heart,
the tears she shed,
a mixture of salt and sorrow,
were collected in the darkness
of her heart.
Drop by drop until her heart
was full --- yet empty.

The tears could not bring
his love closer to her.

WAITING

He is waiting for a love
yet unknown.
Waiting for that touch.
Waiting for that sweet voice
behind a smile to come
and say "I Love You."

Has she been waiting too ?

LOSS AND DESOLATION

It was not the day that broke
--- it was his heart.
For when he woke,
she was no longer there.
The clouds have closed off the sun
and darkness has entered
to seal his days.

The nights, only chilling winds prevail.
The moon, waxed and stripped
of its solitary rounds
--- left an empty sky.
Not one star left to twinkle,
for all have slipped behind a veil:
the vastness of space,
now filled with loneliness.

A thousand thoughts of her
linger in his mind.
The comforts of a loving heart
--- lost for all time,
because, "we really love but once
and we die in that love."*

*Burt Quote

VICTIM OF THE MIND

The morning paper (or should it be
the mourning paper ?) listed him
alphabetically with his fellow travelers,
and his own obituary column said,
"He left this world on such and such a date"
--- stating his accomplishments,
his affiliations and surviving family members,
with a short advertisement for the mortuary
slipped in for good measure.

The trials that were mounting,
the anguish and pain that beset him,
the load on his mind seemed to be
so great, so devastating.
Yet nothing is that critical --- it is only
in the mind that he could no longer cope
--- life testing his strength.
Family member with cancer,
children gone astray, troubling job,
and that old standby, money.

Where was the breaking point ?

Life is so precious,
it is the only thing we really own
--- yet he undertook a permanent solution
to fix a temporary problem
that could have been solved by asking
for help and trusting God.

THE ONENESS LIGHT

We walk through life
in darkness and ignorance
until we meet the One
who holds the light
and has the knowledge.

He will lighten your way,
open your heart and fill it
with oneness.
Then you will become as the light,
to show others the way,
and that inner voice
will speak His truth.

His abundant giving
has become your abundant
love and giving to others
--- to live in the absolute
of God's love
and that will fill your life
to overflowing.

A JEWEL IN THE NIGHT

It was dark and dreary
and he was lost, so he headed
for a blinking neon sign
he glimpsed in the fog
--- it even shimmered in the
rain puddles left on the road.
When he approached,
it was a blue neon cross on a small
old wooden building, paint blistered,
rickety and shabby.
There was joyous singing inside,
so he opened the door and went in
--- everyone stopped, looked around,
acknowledged him and said;
"come in brother, the dark of night
is out there --- the light is here within.
Come join us in that revelation
and the celebration."

That light was a jewel in the night
because it was God's light
that brought him there,
and he is not lost any more.

WAR

*It came like a thief in the night
and stole our souls.
Nightmares haunt our every dream.
Anguish fills our empty hearts
leaving a vacancy in our lives
that can never be filled.
We live with the bruises and the scars
that left us in a cold and silent world,
manipulated, mutilated, amputated.
And we always ask
the question ------ why ?*

*All those wasted lives,
wasted time and energies.
We never can forget the 'Nam we knew
with Napalms, Agent Orange: the rain,
the mud, the pain and all that death
on both sides.
And we always ask
the same question ------ why ?*

>>

Those of us who survived ?
We love our Stars and Stripes
but we still have broken hearts,
shattered dreams
and missing body parts,
and our minds won't let us rest
or set us free.
The others, we left behind in body bags
and carved their names
on a granite wall.

And we always ask
the same question ------ why ?

ETERNAL SEA

Your heart was given to the sea.

Arise ye sleeping sailors
lost in battle and resting in the deep.
The salty sea will reluctantly
give you up and weep.

Remove your shrouds
as a new sunrise gleams.
Be piped aboard to join the crew
of the heavenly ship you'll sail
 --- sail toward that bright Northern light
far from those forgotten seas
you once sailed.

Raise the anchor. Hoist the sails aloft,
trim the riggings, man the braces
and the tiller.
Let the cold wind blow,
billowing the sails as you plow
the wake below your bow,
and the waves wash over your deck.

Peaceful will be your journey
on the eternal sea --- you'll sail
with God's banner flying
from the masthead and a dove
will guide you to His promised shore.

Dedicated to those lost in WWII on the sinking
of the Destroyer DD477 PRINGLE 16 April 1945

CHARLIE'S BULLET

This land was once
a rich green meadow
--- now red stains the green
as foes face each other
in a battle's final scene.

They all dove for cover
and listened to the zings
as enemy shots flew near.
But the one with Charlie's name
was silent to his ear.

The air now still,
no enemy can they hear;
they anxiously wait
for an "all-clear"
to send him down the mountain
to a 'copter standing near.

No trumpets, no Tattoo or Taps.

They will take him home tomorrow
but tonight he holds God's hand,
for he was a gallant soldier
defending his native land.

DREAM GIRL

Each night his dreams
bring her close to him
--- and the night is full of love.
He holds her in fond embrace
as they lie in sweet surrender
until the morning breaks
and she slips away.

He can make it through the day.

Then as the night clouds roll,
his longsome eyes
drift into dream
--- when he rushes to meet her
once again.

LOVER

She may be real
or just a fantasy
--- yet his heart waits
in the night
for her to come
and share his dreams with him.

I ONLY SEE YOU

Looking at a sunset's glow
or the twinkling stars
in the nighttime blue

--- I only see you.

Through the morning mist rising
at a new day dawn, as the sun
dissolves the sparkling dew

--- I only see you.

Each thankful day
exultant eyes ensure
as I wake from sweet dreams

--- dreams where I saw only you.

RUSH AND HURRY WORLD

*In this rush and hurried world
there is so much missed
by not seeing........... Stop,
open your eyes to the beauty
all around you.
There is so much love to be seen
--- be exposed to.*

*An elderly couple on a park bench
holding hands.
A child's tiny fingers clutched
in a loving hand.
Lovers strolling arm in arm.
A little boy loving his dog,
a little girl hugging her doll.
A mother bird tending her nest.*

*Wild flowers growing by the wayside
or through a crack in a sidewalk.
A mirrored lake reflecting the beauty
of a spring day.
A rainbow after a rain --- God's promise.*

*Never be in such a rush and hurry,
and miss the beauty and love
all around you.*

COME SPRING

Our love had grown like ivy
clinging to a wall.
Now, the summer flowers wither
and the leaves will begin to fall.
As these August days are waning,
and the stage is set for fall,
its curtain now descending
 --- September is now on call.

But there is still time for love
and laughter
 --- the deep breathing and the sighs.
Yet these precious days are ending
for I see goodbye in her eyes.

The time will come for parting,
and we'll go our separate way.
I'll hold you dear, deep within my heart
for our love has not seen its day.

Then the cold winds of winter
will fill the lonely days for me,
until the time we are together,
and our spring once more shall be.

COME WINTER

The recent rain washed away
the cold of January,
the sky, now clear and the clouds
 --- puffy white.
February is on the horizon
to celebrate love and hearts.

The March winds blew in
the sweet fragrances of love
as they lay in a fresh green meadow.
During April showers
lightning struck, (so quickly)
and became love's pure light
in his heart.
Now May, and love has bloomed.
She is the center of his heart
 --- his breath of spring.
Gone are the lonely days
and melancholy nights
with unsaid words.
He is now lost in the depth
of her entrancing smile,
reeling from the ecstasy
promised in her passionate eyes.

>>

Desperate to lose all inhibitions
and have their bodies pushed
to conclusion, he holds her
gently in his arms.
Then this love may fade away,
never again to exist in time
 --- come winter, they'll remember !

Burt Quote:
"It's not important where we travel
but what we share along the way."

DESTINY'S PATH

He lost her to her wanderings,
and may never lay in his comfort
or know the love he holds
deep in his heart for her.

She may continue on her way,
but destiny's path will eventually
lead her back to the outstretched arms
of true love.
Then,
wall will tumble, fences will fall
and everything will be opened
and cleared of all obstruction.

In his heart nothing will be denied her
 --- his love will engulf her,
and all her longings and wanderings
will finally be over.

CROSSED PATHS

Her pathways
 --- cluttered with images
of a lost youth, a lost love,
a lost life.
His path
 --- across uncertainty.

Then they met.

They both were blinded
by the light of love.

He broke the seal on his heart
and let love come pouring forth,
and in that love her yearning heart
was laid.

Realizing he wanted her
to be part of his life
more than anything
 --- she became the promise
his heart intends to keep.

UNOBTAINABLE FLAME

On a window sill
*   a candle*
*   flickers.*
A moth
*   flaps its wings*
*   with great*
*   anticipation*
*   --- its heart*
*   beating*
*   an irrevocable tune.*
Fluttering,
*   frightened,*
*   frustrated*
* --- it leaves*
*   wing powder*
smeared
*   on the glass*
* because*
*   the window*
*   was closed*
and it could not
*   reach*
*   the*
*   flame.*

I, that moth.

SEPTEMBER IN PARIS

We used to walk the banks of the Seine
with the shimmering reflection
of Notre Dame in the water
--- browsing through the book
and postcard stalls along the way.
Up to Montmartre, the cathedral
with its panoramic view of the city,
to a sidewalk bistro for a glass of wine,
or over to Rue Pigalle for cabaret
and show.
"The Tower," its dark silhouette
cast against the evening sky;
the luxuriant sounds and sights
never dim in this "city of lights."
Down the Champs–Elysees,
no clocks or time to ponder here
--- only quickened hearts
as September sings its song.

I recall the rainy afternoons
we spent in a quaint café
along the boulevard
as passion strolled the last days
of summer.
Then it was time for us
to cross town to the East terminus
and 'fly away' on the Oriental Express
to a far off sunny shore.

51

GARAGE

You've been there,
with the smell of sweat,
gasoline and diesel,
oil stains on the floor.
There's a waiting room
if you care to wait
  --- with a stack of "freebie" car mags
that came in the mail.
Copies of Time, Reader's Digest
and The Ladies Home Journal
they brought from home, and
faded calendar girls hang on the wall
holding NAPA parts.
It's summer
and a great big fan
is trying to cool off the place.
A fluorescent fixture flickers
  --- almost in time with the music
on the radio.
Just three "good ole' boys"
eking out a living at the B&B Garage.
You can see all the driven miles
on their faces and hands, like tire treads
  --- weathered and worn.
Bryan under the hood of a Chevy.
Richard, under a Benz
up on the lift.
Bill, when he's not doing oil changes,
runs the office.

One with denim sleeves rolled up
to expose an old tattoo of a heart
and Evelyne, whoever Evelyne was.
All three were done one night
in Singapore
 --- Evelyne, Bryan and the tattoo.

With that yellow receipt in hand
you drive away (past a 19whatever
red Ford pick–up out back they use
for weekend fishing trips) knowing,
the job was done right.
So you never have to take a chance
on someone you don't know,
because they treat your car
as if it was their own
 --- and the coffee's good too.

MASK

There is a true face
behind that mask.
There hiding,
so as not to reveal
a vulnerable heart.
She blanks out the longing,
represses emotions and tears
--- to cover fears.

This mask conceals
that side of her;
only true love
can remove that mask
and set her free.

BEHIND THE MASK

When the pretends on the stage of life
are behind you
--- like an actress sit down,
remove the make–up and the mask,
and rejoin the real world.

RESTLESS ONE

Go ahead,
stay on the beach
 --- barefooted,
kicking up sand
 --- picking up stray shells
you'll keep for a while
  to amuse,
     then casually
cast them aside once more.
Wade in and out
of the waves
that only regress
into the sea.

When the sun
and the salt air
have taken their toll
and you find
you're tired of running,
there is a path
over the dunes
that will lead you
back home to me.

HER

My heart, my soul,
my mind and body are in love
with the same person.

I don't want to breath
the air that does not
carry her fragrance.
Nor do I want
to be separated
from her existence
 --- while these old eyes
still behold her.

I would be in hog heaven
if I woke up
and found her
lying next to me
and we had
loved
through
the night.

UNDERNEATH THE BEAUTY

When they see her
and are enthralled
with the beauty and charm
she projects on the surface
--- they don't see the pain
and anguish lurking
just below.
Nor do they sense
the yearnings of her heart.

So, as she dances her mind
allows her to twirl away the past
--- even though some memories
will linger long after the music fades.
Then through trodden time
it will still leave her to weep
the silent tears of longing.

Burt Quote:
"When we leave the past
a new journey begins."

TOMORROW

Tomorrow --- I wait to rise,
to see my future
through these dreamy eyes.

The sounds of the earth emerges,
Nature's music echoing the dawn
of the dew—laden morn, like jewels
--- diamonds glistening upon the grass.

A new day is born.

Every new day we encounter the surging
of our loving hearts: thanking God
for another day.

Burt Quote:
"Before all time has passed us by
recall the beauty of yesterday."

LOVE LOCKED IN A DREAM

Let my dreams be transformed
past that moment of anxiety
into reality.
Break away life's heavy chains
and let them fall.
Let all your fears be swept away
--- accept your vulnerability
as you lay safely in love's embrace.

Let tomorrow bring the answers
that were questions in the night.
And in that tomorrow
walk with me and share my name.

KNELLING OF THE BELLS

When the bells peal
from His distant tower,
let every living thing
hear the ringing
--- listen for their chimes
and answer the call.

Let every heart join the festival
and rejoice.

ETERNAL FESTIVAL

Our souls will grow wings
and fly across the firmament
to reach that distant star
where God has invited us
to His eternal festival.
Not to be found on any celestial charts,
yet the directions can easily be found
deep within our hearts.

BECOMING VISIBLE

I know of a beauty,
so beautiful,
so radiant,
so luminous

.

A love so pure,
so precious.
Many
seek this kind of love,
but never ever
will they find it
until
God
appears

.

THE SOUL'S EYE

The longings
of the human heart
will cease
when the soul's eye
sees God.

ATTITUDE HEALING

If we do not have
attitude healing
we are left with
an empty heart,
an abandoned soul
and a lost life.

Let us heal together !

STOIC MOMENT

The waves surge toward the shore
then mellow into foam
sliding across the darkened sand.
Then they seem to come to rest,
desisting the process of motion
before returning to become
the next surging wave.

That precious moment,
that microcosmic second
of stillness
is what we all strive for
and want to bathe in.

YESTERDAY'S LOVE

The winds of change
can blow chillingly.
The enchantment of candles
can flicker out and summer love
can grow cold and dark.
But come winter
their warm, young hearts
can make the fireside glow.

Yet I ask,
is their love still as wonderful
as yesterday ?
The clouds, all passed
--- the sun is bright.
For him, he glows
with the rise of morning
when he awakes and sees her face.

But is their love
as meaningful as yesterday ?

FAR FROM PEERING EYES

On a secluded island beach
somewhere far from peering eyes
and the world,
the golden sand clings
to their naked bodies
as they bask in the sun,
but the heat is from their own passion.
The palm trees sway in rhythm
with his fingers caressing her
as a tropical breeze tries in vain
to cool their lust.
The dolphins tenderly shriek,
heads bobbing up and down
 --- their way of saying, yes ! yes !

Engulfed in pleasure, their shapes
captured in pools their bodies made
in the sand as the waves subside.

Angel wings in the sand above.
Devil's triangle below.

ALL THE WAY HOME

It's the bottom of the ninth:
the home team
is at a home game.
The score is tied,
with two men on,
as our last hope
steps up to the plate.

Tension mounts
as the visiting pitcher
stretches, looks around,
hesitates --- winds and throws
 --- "clink,"
the ball rises, arching high
across the field
and over the fence.

We all walk home with pride,
through the spilt coke cups
and scattered popcorn,
as fireworks burst in the sky.

IMPERSONATOR

Elvis is alive at a downtown
Memphis night club ?

His fake hair, dark glasses
 --- that caped white sequin jumpsuit
that fits too close 'cause he's fat.
That wiggle, the snapping of the knee
 --- well rehearsed.
Elvis he's not,
yet he thinks with all the trappings
maybe he can pull it off.
"No way Jose,"
we laugh and enjoy the entertainment
 --- and as his act is over, a voice
on the PA system announces
"Elvis has left the building."
Tomorrow night he'll try again
to create the Elvis image
with a different crowd.

His "Graceland" is an efficiency
down the street; he walks to work
 --- but nobody notices.
Then once a year he emerges in Las Vegas
to compete in a sea of Elvis' for a prize.

Relinquishing the facade, he may have been
a success in his own right.

How sad !

HERMIT

He lives in the mountains,
a hermit to himself,
and walks in the glory
of all of God's creations.

Free to feel the seasons' change
--- to smell the fragrance
of the trees and flowers,
to bathe in the cool streams
of summer
--- to enjoy the glowing colours
of autumn.
Free to walk
in the white snows of winter
into the soft spring rains
that bring everything
back to life.

He relishes in his companionship
with the Lord, and praises
all that He has created.

He lives in the mountains,
a hermit to the outside world.

DEPARTURE

He lost track of time
and yesterday's memories
seem to have slipped
from his mind
as life presses itself
against him --- wanting
to take him away
from his worn out hopes
and lost dreams.

Soon his longings
will be silent.
Free from his crumbling past
he'll wander off
onto a mountain
covered with snow,
and vanish into the white.

SUNLIGHT SHADOWS

Summer love
was the source of their pleasure,
a time they will always treasure.

Now summer's gone
and autumn begins
to shoulder its seasonal round.
The fall leaves begin to cover
the verdant ground.

The setting sunlight shadows
trace across the barren meadow
waiting for the first signs of snow
 --- and leaves their day
with golden glow.

SPRING'S SONG

The clear blue skies of spring shine
as love awakens once more
to fill the air with birdsongs,
love songs and poetry.
My darling,
come fill my heart
with spring's promises
and walk with me
through the rain's clarity
that bathes everything
in beauty and pure light.

Let us linger in love
until summer's eyes
begin to close,
and love approaches
its winter bed
to blanket in repose
until the first notes
of a spring song
are heard,
and love
is awakened again.

WAITING FOR HER

The hours fall away
into days waiting for her.
His heart keeps ticking
with expectancy
of her home—coming.

He has unfastened times latch
and opened tomorrows door.
For the billowing clouds
have parted and the colours
of autumn blaze in all their glory
as he waits for her
--- hoping before the first blast
of winter comes to chill his bones
and freeze his heart, she comes.

ENDLESSLY WAITING

She cannot hide from him
behind her facade,
the make–up and locks of golden hair.
He has known her with her soul exposed,
without her make–up and fancied hair.
He knows the deep wounds
that may never heal,
the hurting that still burns,
the pain that she tries to shield.

He has a love that binds his heart to her.
He cherishes the gifts she gave him
without knowing
--- for she put her trust in him
and it changed his life for the better.
She won his devotion
yet she declined his heart.
Her love still eludes him,
and he is endlessly waiting and wanting
what her heart is not now
willing to share.

He knows the inner loveliness of her,
the spark of love that will set her free.
Therefore he will always be there,
loving her with an open heart,
even when she is old and gray
and her eyes have lost their luster.

She will never hear his goodbye song.

SECRETLY HE LOVES

His heart keeps a secret
and languishes
for the absence of her.
She is his night—dream Queen
 --- touching his soul
with her lambent light.

Although there are barriers
that keep them apart
 --- though she be imprisoned
with her self—imposed solitude,
never willing to be obligated
to anyone's servitude.

Through evening shadows
he yearns for her to come
 --- distain the night,
un—fetter her bonds
and remove her repined desires,
the despair and anguish
that has held her at bay
and let the love—goddess
inside emerge.

Time to let her soul
be golden dres't
 --- to let her adoring heart
be the one to reign,
to comfort and soothe
her constant pain.

GOLDEN DAYS, SILVER NIGHTS

The distant shadows call.
The night's darkness hides
   all the broken pieces of heart
   love has left lying in the dust.

Gone are the silver clouds
   and silver moon that enchanted
   their nights.

All the times they shared,
   now just a memory.
Lost, for time will not renew
   those golden moments
   and golden days that filled
   their lives with joy.

LOST IN SEPARATION

He is so far lost
in a spiritual love
that he can never be
retrieved.

She is beauty, she is love
and he embraces this.
Day after day,
night after night
 --- through the weeks
 --- across the months,
year after year
he sits and dreams and loves.
Yet she did not become a reality,
only existing in his consciousness
as a dream.
This separation from her
is the hardest thing his heart
has ever had to endure.

His cup, still empty.
His candle, beginning to flicker
in a pool of molten wax
 --- soon to be extinguished,
and this love will cease to exist
in this life.
Know that he will take it with him
into the next --- waiting.

So don't weep.

EMPTY NIGHT

The thoughts of the day
  have passed,
  the fleeting words,
  no longer remembered.
The images stored
  in the mind's–eye
  --- now faded.
Life's tedium's
  laid aside.
Silence begins to loom
  through consciousness
  --- time to gather ourselves
  into the safety of solitude
  to reflect, meditate and pray.

Most of the night is empty
  --- we have to fill it with dreams.

THE ART OF LETTING GO

Dance with the wind.
Twirl like a dervish
until you disappear
with delight into self.
Then you will be at oneness
with the One
and experience the gifts
of peace, love and joy.

PATHWAY

Never let my wandering feet
tread in darkness,
but always in my pathway
--- Your light to shine on me.

May You always be there
to light my way.

Lord, lead me in faith and love,
and may my pathway
be the righteous one
so I can join those who have
traveled there before me
--- and forever find my peace.

SHRINE

His love shattered
and left lying in the dust.

He gathered
all the pieces of his heart
and built a shrine
to that love.

MEMORIAL

He will build a memorial
to love in her name
 --- then
lay down beside it
and die.

SANCTUARY OF TEARS

Tears now fill his sanctuary
crying with a voice
  --- thick with pain.
She is lost from him
  --- yet she is still loved.

As the day wanes
and slips into the quietude of night
  --- dark clouds gather
and cover the moon's path
  --- darkness seals their past.

When time moves into morning
  --- there is no sleep
for nothing will still or heal
his lost and lonely heart.

A NEW HOME

They were wandering, searching for
their souls a place to rest
--- their weary bodies to take refuge.
for their journey has been long
and hard.

Then God stepped in to provide
a place for them in the universe.
It was known to them from the start,
but they had not discovered it,
or how to get there --- it was love.

Now together with heart, mind, soul
and body joined, they have found
their new home.
A place only a few achieve
--- so many only dream about
--- the ultimate love, as they settle
into forever together.

Lovers, friends, companions
--- evermore.

DIAMOND

Although love had burned away
leaving his life in ashes,
through the blackness of his days
he rambled, endlessly
 --- searching.

While sifting through
a world of cinders
 --- dark and cold,
he found a diamond
pure in brilliance,
flawless in beauty.

His days of darkness over
 --- his longings subsided,
as he claimed her
for his own.

Burt Quote:
"A stone heart crushed by tons of love
becomes a diamond."

LIFE–JOINING

The warmth of the summer night air
surrounds them as they sit
listening to music and indulging
in red wine.
They had evolved, come together,
in such a relaxed and loving relationship.
No pretense or inhibitions
 --- they know where they came from,
they know where they are going.

Undressing their thoughts
and themselves,
they approach the bed
 --- as old lovers do,
with a sense of reverence.

Lying there so close beside her
 --- he asked himself:
"Why had he come so far,
lived so long without her ?"
He feels the emptiness of years
dwindle in her arms.
The tenderness, the love
he was once denied
 --- now abounds.

>>

The warmth of their bodies
transport them to the next level
of consciousness during that moment
of complete surrender.

There they finally realize
that love is just a word used
to express many feelings,
many things --- and life–joining
is the ultimate plateau
of their being.

LOST ON A MOONLIT BEACH

He remembers the night
they spent together
on that moonlit beach.
Lying there in flesh and bone,
joined together as one
in the cool morning mist
 --- vapor rising
from their exhausted frames.
They had surrendered
to the enchantment,
the moonlight,
the star–filled night,
and the soothing waves.

One sweet night of ecstasy
passed all existence
 --- reaching beyond the deepest
part of the universe
with love merging
as a new morning star.

But when the dawn rose
she was no longer there.
Now he asks their star
 --- does she also remember ?

A REMINDING HEART

He fights the night dreams,
  the day memories
  of her.
They come to him
  through the shadows
  and at unexpected moments
  when something
  reminds him of her.

Pigeons in the park
  they use to feed
  --- a child snuggling
  its tattered doll.
That fading rainbow
  they ran under
  after a spring rain.
That cozy café by candlelight,
  their favorite movie
  --- their favorite song.
Those warm nights
  they'd strolled barefooted
  along a beach by moonlight.

He clings to these memories
  --- they keep him alive
  until the time he joins her.

ANTICIPATION

The table is set.
The flowers and tapers
arranged just so.
Your favorite wine
is being chilled
 --- I wait.

Enter with all your
graceful beauty,
causing the quickening
of my heart.
Fill the room
with your sweet fragrance
 --- your heavenly glow
that lights my darkness.

The candles also wait.

REMEMBER TOO, THIS LOVE

When the sweetness of our song
comes to ear --- remember me.

Other hearts may hold you.
Other loves enfold you
--- yet I will remember you.

The years will pass,
and your blood will run cold,
your eyes go dim and your hair
turn silver-gray
--- I will still remember.

As long as there are flowers in the field
and diamonds sparkling in the sky
--- I will remember.

At night in your moment of prayer,
remember --- as I remember.

And when summer colours turn
to autumn hues --- remember too,
this love now faded.

DRIFTING, WAITING

Awhile, in my silent boat
with muffled oars,
drifting towards
those golden shores
--- I wait.
The earth may quake
and tremble
with darkness close at hand
and the waves of death
surround --- I wait.
But, I will have no fear
for the Lord will speed me
on my way,
and I will smoothly sail
on to His promised land.

BRIDGING MEMORIES

The new span and its impressive sight
--- an engineering marvel composed
in concrete, steel and cables
arching across the river.
Yet you'll miss the old steel bridge
--- with its towering structure
of lattice design,
and the elements rusting away
its dark green coat.

Now only photographs remain.

There were those rare,
peaceful moments it afforded
when the barriers went down
and the center went up
waiting for a tall ship
to come sliding through.
Out of the car and onto the rail
to take in the expansive view.

Then the center came down,
the barriers lifted
and you traveled across its span
back into the hectic world.

THE FIRST LADY

The White House has gleamed
with many First Ladies,
from Abigail Adams to the present,
who have pressed their charm and grace
into all it encompasses
and endured their cherished tenure
in that grand old house
 --- making it home.

WANDERING MINSTREL

In the highland's Northern light
white-washed cottages
gleam in the twilight glow
that never turns full night.

Singing and strumming
on his merry way,
a wandering minstrel
strolls through the land
--- across windswept moors,
mountain peaks and vistas grand,
through the beautiful heather
caressing his beloved Scotland.

Serenading with mystical tales
of ancient warriors, singing songs
of enamored hearts, star–crossed lovers,
and their ghostly echoes whispering
in the night.

Inside an isolated crofter's cottage
with its warming hearth aglow,
is where he will ask for refuge
from the damp and cold of night.

At dawn to rise and continue
his wandering in the new day light.

GALLANTRY'S HORSE

He rode his great white steed
at break—neck speed
 --- its nostrils swell
as smoke expels,
and hoofs come crashing
to the ground
with a thunderous roar,
and clouds of dust
billowing behind
as they plow the night
 --- in flight
to a fair maiden's rescue.

TWO–COLOURED MOON

Up and full
--- full of love's light.
Its crisp, alabaster glow
radiates onto the earth
at a time when young hearts
dance through nights of delight.

The other, cold and gray
 --- like tarnished silver,
veiled in smoke–coloured clouds
that shadow life
at their time of parting.

SHADOW

At eleven a.m.
it starts to diminish.
Walk slowly at noon
so you'll keep
your shadow underfoot.

At one p.m. it begins
to rise again, growing
longer and longer
'til sunset.

Walk with your shadow
behind you --- that way
you'll always walk
in the light.

SHAGGIN' FEET

The sandy shore,
the rolling waves,
those sunny summer days
on the Boulevard
 --- along the boardwalk,
are gone.

Body now lost,
hair now gray,
but these feet
are still "shaggin'
the night away."

When these Weejuns® are tired
and a hole breaks through the sole,
and that copper penny
turns black,
I will hang them up
and won't look back.

I'll shag right out of this world.

There will be another
Myrtle Beach somewhere
 --- a place like Fat Harold's
Ducks, and all the rest,
where DJ's play
those familiar songs all day.
I'll be waiting there for you to come
and shag once more with me.

SNOW ROSE

The morning light breaks
  shining down below
  on a spring garden
  --- shimmering dewdrops glow.

Two lovers there entwined
  among the blossoming flowers
  --- love's seeds they sown.

Sweetly do the days fly past,
  and in the white of winter
  a single rose will grow.

PEARLS OF RAIN

Pearls of rain,
upon my window pane
--- stream down
to join each other in dance.

They twirl around like dervishes,
pirouetting to the ground
--- then the rain–music stops,
and they vanish without a sound.

LOSING IT ?

Sitting at the edge
of madness, caught up
in the struggle
between sanity and insanity
 --- contemplating his next move:
to continue loving
or let them bring "The Jacket"
and take him away ?

Between the loneliness of his days
and the looming dark of night,
he hears her voice and their music
coming from somewhere within.
He sees love through bleary eyes
 --- and it is she.

Although this love
is unrequited he listens
to what his heart mandates,
and keeps returning.

LOST IN A CAVE

Shadows trace across
the paradise he once knew.
His heart, soaked
from springtime tears.
His garment, drenched
from April showers
was once as smooth as fine silk
--- now threadbare sackcloth.
Life, once full of limpid wine
--- now only dregs remain.
The saffron sun, bright
during his days and nights
--- now descended into darkness.

His heart, an empty cave
where blackness hangs
from the ceiling and reeks
from a love --- now dead.

No light to penetrate the darkness,
no hope for recovery.

Love and life lost.

RELENTLESS MOON

Sad, but relentlessly
the moon travels nightly,
ignoring the passage of the seasons
 --- contemplating its own changes
 --- its perennial cycles.

Ever to rise and ark,
come to full bloom
 --- only to become a sliver
of light in the sky
once more.
Its mood, ever changing,
from brilliant white
to mysterious gray.

Man has walked on its surface
in our lifetime.

Will it ever be the same ?

It will always
cast a spell on lovers
and fascinate astronomers.

FEARFUL TONGUE

Fear steals his tongue
as he tries to say I love you.

Fear of rejection.
Fear of acceptance.

Every time he tries to speak
of such things as love,
his tongue gets in the way
 --- so he turns to his pen
to voice his thoughts
of love
 --- and sends them on their way.

And she always replies

"Yes, I know."

RICH IN HEART

She has taken his heart
  with her infectious smile.
Tempered his soul
  with that angelic voice.
O God, how he loves her.
She graces him in dance,
  breaks him out in love
  and puts him in a trance.
His love life was in poverty
  'til they met, now he is
  the richest man in heart.

A WILLOW WEEPS

A weeping willow
sheds its tears
and joins him
in his sorrow.
Although she has gone
this day --- will she
return tomorrow ?

QUEEN OF HEARTS

My life was like a deck of cards.

Just numbers and symbols
  on a playing field
  with faces unknown to me
  --- a gallery of stately portraits
  until fate
  dealt me the Queen of Hearts.

*

HEART'S DOOR

When you open the door
to your heart
I'll be there standing
at its threshold.

SUNDAY MORNING

From her dream–state
she called to him in a voice
so sweet and low,
"come cuddle with me."

In a moment of serenity,
they lay in love's embrace.
He kissed the nape of her neck
for he knew it wouldn't be long
before his "star" would dim
and fade away.

As the sun's rays
slowly broke through
announcing the new day
 --- she was gone.

SILENT SOLITUDE

How peaceful the solitude
of early morning as I lie there quietly
--- so very quiet.

With my mind's eye I generate
an image of her --- taking a deep breath
and listen to my heart's rapid beat.

Suddenly I feel her presence
as a lone dove's coo
breaks the silence
of its own solitude.

I enjoy the illusion.

GYPSY SOUL

He has roamed this world
with gypsy feet.
He has seen life and love winning,
and seen them in defeat.
Hearts full of love and joy,
hearts lonely and lost, even worse,
his in particular
 --- it must be his gypsy curse.

If love would come to him
and finally take hold,
it would surely save
this gypsy soul.

DIMMING FIRE

The dimming of the fire,
  the dwindling of the flame,
  the smoke ribbon's curl
   --- ceases to ascend,
  and love is lost
  among the ashes.

The days will lose
  their warmth
  and the chilling air descend.
And love,
  never to be rekindled
  once the dimming
  fire begins.

CONSUMED

Love consumed me
*   as I took your hand*
*   and placed it in mine.*

Now the sky is full
*   of silver clouds,*
*   and the diamonds*
*   of evening sparkle*
*   from deepest space.*

CAN I FLEE or HIDE ?

Can the antelope
flee the fire
raging on the plain
* --- the rabbit*
burrow deep enough in the ground
to conceal itself from the hawk ?

Can I flee the fire in my heart
or hide from the love
that would consume me ?

THE TRANQUIL HOURS

No news of death and destruction.
No absurd television sitcoms.
No heavy traffic or road rage,
or bad weather to contend with.

A slow walk through the countryside
where peace can be felt
along every pathway.
The beauty and the sounds of nature
reassure you that God
is walking beside you
in these tranquil hours.

SELF TRAVELER

"Don't go where the path may lead.
Go instead where there is no path
and leave a trail."
         Ralph Waldo Emerson
              1803–1882.

He never followed
the well trodden path
 --- but always made
a new path of his own.
He had traveled a long road
with its many ups and downs
 --- but he has loved the ride,
it has been fruitful,
full of hopes and dreams.

At times standing
on the roadside
to catch his breath,
when his heart
felt love or loss
 --- but never to loosing his way.

When he reaches that final
mile—marker on his journey
he will see the light
beyond death's shadow
and his soul will be
at peace.

HIS SONG

I awoke
and heard His song
and ran to be there
before the dawn
of rising sun.

Today all was revealed
when with my God
--- my love was sealed.

So tender are the sighs
(the sighs of relief)
caressing my heart
with truth, not lies.

At my sun's
last setting hour,
I will leave this world
to be with His Son.

THISBE AND PYRAMUS

He loved her in secret,
in secret she loved him too.
They tryst'd outside Babylon's walls
so they could be together.
Near the tomb of Ninus
--- where they always met,
he found her blood–stained garment
--- left behind as she fled a lioness
in her path.
Thinking she was dead,
his heart rent, so heavy,
his love so deep --- killed himself*
out of remorse.

Thisbe, realizing his deed,
knowing his great love --- joined him.

What a great love they had.
*It is always better to check first
before taking any drastic action.

RIVER OF LOVE

We have come a long way
since that eventful day
when our two hearts met,
yet walls have been built
to protect your heart.

There is a river of love flowing.
On its bank you still sit hesitant
--- with the fear of crossing.

Be vulnerable. Swim this river.
You won't sink or drown,
for true love will keep you afloat.

Reaching the other shore
I'll be there with open arms.

SEAFARER COMIN' HOME

I missed you once my darlin',
I miss you nar again.
For I am comin' home to thee
 --- nev'r again to roam
the deep blue sea.

The winds a–blowin'
strong my darlin'
and billowin'–up my sail.
So, I'll be home by the dawnin'
 --- in thy harbor
my heart to anchor.

Open your arms my darlin'
 --- open your arms to me
for I am comin' home my darlin'
nev'r to leave
for the sea, from thee.

I'll make you my bride my darlin'
 --- I'll make you my precious bride.

>>

We'll build a little cottage by the sea
and there we will reside.
We'll sit and watch the sunset
as it sets across the land,
and we will watch
our tomorrows as they rise
from beyond the sea.

DEW DROP

I an but a dew drop
on the leaf of life.

*

ANY MOMENT

Like that dangling leaf
ready to drop from the tree
--- my life goes fast.
So I live each day
as if it were my last.

*

DROP OFF

I could drop off into sleep
and never know I was gone.

TO DIE AND LIVE AGAIN

The afternoon sky,
cloudless and transparent
--- you can see infinity.

The September embers
with their amber glow
follow autumn's flame
as the leaves turn and fall
to adorn the darkened earth
with umber, sepia, red and gold.
Testimony to life
evolving, revolving
--- dying to live again.

The final sweetness
of the season beckons me
to sleep, to sleep,
and I too, shall die
to live again.

OPPOSITES

1.
LIFE is a parade
with marching bands,
a multilayer of colours
--- the beauty of the world
passing in review.
You try to catch
all the coins
and confections
as they are thrown
your way.

2.
DEATH is a motorcade
with organ music and quietude,
a processional through the park
 --- dressed in black.
A moment of remembrance.

Now they thoughtfully
bring you flowers.

TOUCHED BY TIME

Touched by time
* the hours go fast.*
With God blessing
* another year has passed.*
Another year slips
* into oblivion*
* with the echoes of the past*
* still haunting our thoughts.*
The multi–colours of time
* we wove into the tapestry*
* of our yesterday's.*
The music, the sadness,
* the joy and love*
* we have known*
* through the year.*

Now we begin to nurture
* with that breath of anticipation*
* --- the next new dawn*
* and tomorrow.*
So always have
* peace within your soul,*
* love in your heart,*
* a twinkle in your eye*
* and a prayer on your lips.*

THANK YOU GOD

Thank you God for helping me
in my yesterdays
and allowing me tomorrows.
Thank you God for being there
through all my joys and sorrows.

My life that You have turned around,
has been a revelation.
Thank you God I know you're there,
to guide and watch over me.
Your love is my salvation.

MY CIRCULATION PRINCIPLE

When I apply
my "circulation principle"
I expend energy
and I energize others.
When I give comfort,
I am blessed two–fold,
once by giving
--- once by receiving.
When I offer friendship and love
and it is received and returned,
I know my "CP" is working.
When I exert my optimism
the world around me
seems brighter --- my task lighter.
When I include others in my prayers,
a blessing and/or healing
takes place in each of our lives.

Turning to God for answers,
I find my "circulation principle"
is working for me every day
--- in every way, and I share
in the abundance that flows
through my life.

"Give, and it will be given to you
--- for the measure you give will be
the measure you get in return."
                    LUKE 6:38

"In the end these three things
matter most:
How well did you love ?
How full did you love ?
How deeply did you learn to let go ?"
THE BUDDHA
c563–c483BC
India

Also by the Author

POETRY My Never Ending
Dance With Words
ISBN No. 1–4120–0031–9

LOVE and SUMMER DAYS
FADE AWAY
ISBN No. 1–4120–1126-4

Share A Tender Moment
Includes
"We Walked The Heathered Meadows"
A poetic journey through Scotland.
ISBN No. 1–4120–6586–0

OF ROSES and SPLIT WINE
ISBN No. 1–4120–6587–9

RED PENNED DIARY
ISBN No. 1–1420–6588–7

Order these books online at www.trafford.com
or email orders@trafford.com
Also available at BARNES&NOBLE amazon.com INGRAM
and through local bookhandlers.

ABOUT THE AUTHOR

Mr. Pringle is a native of Savannah, Georgia
who resides in Jacksonville, Florida. He is an artist,
architectural designer and watercolorist.
His artwork is included in many private and
corporate collections and the official Florida
Bicentennial book. "Born of the Sun" contains two
of his paintings.
He has published many volumes of poetry and his
work is included in several anthologies and on
spoken word CD's.
His biography is included in Who's Who in
American Art, Marquis Who's Who in the South.
The Cambridge (England) Dictionary of
International Biography and is also included
in International Men of Achievement.
He has designed several United States postage
stamps and has received 21 Honorariums from
the United Nations for his graphic postal designs.
PBS/WJXT produced a half hour segment
about his graphic designing.
Burt is also an accomplished ballroom dancer.

N.N. Wood